Camdean School

KU-067-979

Item no.   01355

KING HORACE'S TREASURE HUNT

Written by
Quentin Flynn

Illustrated by
Ian Forss

PROPERTY OF

29 MAR 2004

HORWITZ
MARTIN

Contents

Chapter 1

King Horace The Hopeless

King Horace the Hopeless was in a bad mood. He had to pay some treasure to his neighbour, King Roger the Ruthless. If he paid the treasure every year, King Roger would promise not to take his lands.

King Horace the Hopeless and Oliver, his Prime Minister, sat in the castle's treasure room. Most of the treasure chests were empty.

"We don't have much treasure, do we?" asked the king sadly.

"No, your Majesty," said Oliver.

"What can we do?" cried the king. "Roger the Ruthless will take my lands if I don't pay him any treasure. I won't be a king anymore!"

"Send some men on a treasure hunt," suggested Oliver. "Send them to South America. I have heard there are many treasures there!"

"Good idea," said the king. "I'm glad *I* thought of that! Who has a ship?"

Oliver scratched his head.

"Eldred has a ship," he suggested.

"Yes!" said the king. "Eldred! He has a ship, you know!"

"Yes, your Majesty," sighed Oliver.

Chapter 2

A Treasure Hunt

Eldred and the ship's crew came to the castle. The king handed Eldred a scroll and told him to read it.

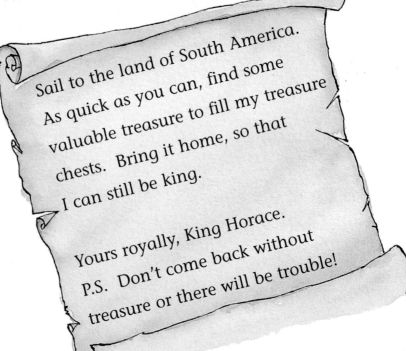

Sail to the land of South America. As quick as you can, find some valuable treasure to fill my treasure chests. Bring it home, so that I can still be king.

Yours royally, King Horace. P.S. Don't come back without treasure or there will be trouble!

Eldred bowed. "I will be happy to help you," he said.

King Horace the Hopeless nodded. "Off you go. We don't have much time."

Eldred and his crew marched back to his ship. Crowds of people cheered and waved. The people knew that Eldred and his crew were going to help their king.

Chapter 3

A Sack Of Dust

King Horace the Hopeless was feeling both excited and nervous. One month passed. Two months passed. Three months passed. Finally, Eldred and his crew sailed back into the port. The king jiggled on his throne. He bit his nails.

"Tell Eldred to come here at once," he ordered. "Wait!" he added. "Tell him to have a bath first. He might be smelly after months on a ship."

"Yes, your Majesty," replied Oliver.

Soon after his bath, Eldred stood before the king.

"Well?" asked King Horace. "How many horses and carts will you need to unload my treasure from your ship?"

"None, your Majesty," replied Eldred, smiling. "Your treasure is in this sack."

He placed a small sack at the king's feet.

The king looked at it. He poked it with his foot.

"There's not much gold in there,"
said King Horace.

"No, your Majesty. There's something much
better than gold," said Eldred.

The king frowned. "No gold? What, then?"

Eldred smiled. He opened the sack, and the
king looked inside. There was nothing but
brown dust in the sack! The king looked at the
brown dust and then at Eldred.

"A sack of brown DUST?" he shouted. "I ask for treasure and you give me a sack of brown dust?"

"N-no, n-no," stammered Eldred. "This is not dust, your Majesty. This is called 'xocolatl'. It is South American treasure. You eat it!"

"Eat it? It's dust!" yelled the king. "I wanted treasure, you fool!"

He told a soldier to take Eldred away.

"Cut off his head," said the king.

"We're not allowed to do that anymore," whispered Oliver.

"Aren't we?" asked the king. "Feed him to the lions, then!"

"We don't have lions anymore," whispered Oliver.

"Don't we?" asked the king. "Do we still have a dungeon?"

"Yes, your Majesty," nodded Oliver.

"Good!" smiled the king. "Throw him in the dungeon!"

Just then, Roger the Ruthless arrived at the castle. He was one day early!

Chapter 4

King Roger The Ruthless

"Roger the Ruthless is at the castle gates, your Majesty," whispered Oliver.

"Let him in," groaned King Horace. "I'll see him at dinner time for our royal feast. I hope he's in a good mood."

Downstairs, in the kitchen, the cooks started cooking the royal feast. Meat roasted over big fires. Vegetables boiled and bubbled in huge pots. Freshly baked loaves of bread were taken out of the oven. Fresh fruits were washed.

In the middle of the kitchen, Carlos, the dessert cook, quickly stirred his dessert mix. He was worried. His oven wasn't working very well.

Upstairs, King Horace the Hopeless welcomed King Roger the Ruthless.

"You really should visit more often," King Horace said politely.

"Maybe I will," said King Roger impolitely. "Do you have my treasure?"

"Well, um ... we'll talk about that later," said King Horace. "Let's have a royal feast first!"

King Roger and King Horace sat down at the royal table. King Roger grabbed a large piece of meat and started to eat. King Horace didn't eat anything.

"Is something wrong?" asked King Roger.

"No," replied King Horace quietly. "Everything's just fine!" But it wasn't. He felt ill. And downstairs, in the kitchen, something terrible had just happened.

Downstairs, Carlos was very upset. His oven had just broken down.

"Why did it break down NOW?" he cried. "The king will throw me in the dungeon! My desserts are not cooked properly. They have not turned brown yet!"

Chapter 5

Dessert Disaster

Carlos looked at the pale desserts. Then he had an idea.

"Soldiers!" he yelled. "Find me something brown that I can put on these desserts. They *must* look cooked!"

The soldiers rushed off and searched the castle for something brown. Carlos sat with his head in his hands.

Within a few minutes, one soldier returned with a small sack from the king's room.

"This is the brown dust that the treasure hunters brought back from South America," he said. "It was all we could find."

"Can you eat it?" asked Carlos, as he looked at the brown dust. The soldier shrugged his shoulders.

"The treasure hunters said it could be eaten," he replied.

Carlos had no choice. He grabbed a handful of the brown dust. Then he sprinkled it over his pale desserts. The soldiers carried the desserts upstairs. Carlos sat in the kitchen, hoping the kings would not notice how terrible his desserts were.

Upstairs, King Roger licked his lips.

"Where's dessert?" he burped.

A soldier put the two brown desserts in front of the kings.

King Roger picked up a whole dessert and ate it in one gulp. Suddenly, he stopped. His eyes opened wide. He licked his lips again. He looked at King Horace.

Chapter 6

A Huge Party

"What IS this?" he asked, smiling. "It's the most delicious dessert I've ever eaten."

King Horace looked surprised and sniffed a dessert. Oliver whispered into his ear. Then, King Horace smiled, too. "*This* is your treasure," he said. "Do you like it?"

"Like it?" shouted King Roger. "I LOVE it! What's it called?"

"Xocolatl," said King Horace. He looked at Oliver. "Or was it cox-alot-l? Or cho-col-axel?"

"Did you say 'cho-co-late'? Chocolate?"
King Roger ate the other dessert. He slapped
King Horace on the back. "It's better than any
treasure you've paid me before," he said.

Later that evening, a huge party was held in the castle. During the party, King Horace spoke to Oliver about Eldred.

"Is Eldred still in the dungeons?" asked the king.

"Yes," whispered Oliver.

"It was lucky I didn't have his head cut off or feed him to the lions!" said the king.

"Yes, your Majesty," smiled Oliver.

"Bring him here right away!" ordered
King Horace. "Eldred is about to receive the
best prize. I will make him SIR Eldred!"

And he did:

Sir Eldred, Official Chocolate Supplier to King Horace the Hopeless and King Roger the Ruthless!